Socrates' Wild Ocean Adventure

Book One: The Adventure Begins

Tom McGee

iUniverse, Inc.
New York   Bloomington

Socrates' Wild Ocean Adventure
Book One: The Adventure Begins

iUniverse books may be ordered through booksellers or by contacting:

iUniverse
1663 Liberty Drive
Bloomington, IN 47403
www.iuniverse.com
1-800-Authors (1-800-288-4677)

ISBN: 978-1-4401-6755-3 (sc)
ISBN: 978-1-4401-6753-9 (dj)
ISBN: 978-1-4401-6754-6 (ebk)

Printed in the United States of America

iUniverse rev. date: 9/17/2009

Contents

Chapter One

Socrates was sad. He had started his day with his sister Mara, a beautiful cod with a long, sleek, powerful body. She had recently been afflicted with a strange illness, seemingly caused by a recent change in the water where she lived; sores were starting to appear on her sides, and she was frequently complaining of feeling sick. As a loyal brother, Socrates stayed by her side constantly. He was daily scouring the shorelines, trying to find the source of the pollution affecting their home, which was near the mouth of the Aegean Sea. His travel was always limited, though, because Mara was continually getting weaker. He had noticed on several occasions that large vessels would dump their sewage and garbage straight into the sea. In addition, he had heard from pelagic fish, which are transient by nature, about sewage pouring right into the sea from sources on land.

Now he was at the peak of his frustration, and Mara was struggling in a huge drift net to get free—Socrates himself barely escaped by flopping over the top edge of the net; he had tried desperately to nudge Mara over the edge, too, but the action of the net proved to be too fast and too strong. Not knowing what else to do, he grabbed a rope hanging over the side of the boat, clinched it in his teeth, and managed to slip it through an opening in the net; then, he grabbed the end of the rope, headed straight for the propeller shaft, and swam a couple of times around it, forming a loop. When the captain restarted the engines and put the boat in gear, the rope wound itself around the propeller shaft, which in turn sucked the net into the propeller blades, yanking a bunch of the fishing gear off the boat. The propeller jammed so badly that the vessel completely lost propulsion, and the motor started overheating.

The captain screamed at the deckhands. "How can you be so stupid? I told all of you idiots at least a thousand times: never leave anything hanging over the edge!"

In a rage, he grabbed one of the deckhands by the back of the neck and the seat of his pants and hurled him overboard. "You moron!" he yelled. "You're not coming back on board until that mess is unraveled!"

The captain then, in his fit of rage, proceeded to throw two more of the deckhands over the side to help with the propeller. However, the situation of the boat was dire—the craft was now only a few hundred feet away from running onto the rocks that lined the western edge of the sea—so the crewmembers' efforts were an exercise in futility. There was no way to save the boat in time. The current was strong, and the bow of the vessel slammed into a jagged rock pile. The boat quickly filled with water, and all hands on board abandoned ship. As the vessel slipped below the surface, Socrates raced around, examining the part of the net that was still stuck on the deck of the boat. He was looking for his sister.

"Mara!" he yelled. "Where are you?"

A faint voice pierced the silence: "Socrates!"

Socrates finally found his sister. He saw the tangled net tightly wrapped around her. He started crying and tenderly apologizing for failing her. "Oh, Mara, I'm so sorry. *Please* forgive me. I should have known to stay closer to the rocks this morning. Oh, Sis, I am so sorry. Please forgive me!"

Mara focused her eyes directly into his and, in a struggling whisper, managed to say, "My dear brother, it's not your fault. I did not have much time left anyway. Just know that I love you. You were always my hero and protector." Her eyes then slowly closed, and she faded into the silence of death.

Socrates had never experienced such a void in his life; his poor sister was gone. As he glanced around, he saw the captain grabbing onto a rock, trying to climb from the water. Socrates quickly reacted: he darted toward the captain in a rage and struck him in the side with his snout, knocking him back into the water, and then he opened his powerful jaws and sank his teeth into one of the man's flailing arms. The man started crying in panic and pain. However, he still had one arm free—Socrates temporarily released his grip when the captain hit him hard with his fist. Nevertheless, this episode was not over; Socrates fiercely reemerged from the water with his jaws wide open, face-to-face with his victim. Socrates' steely stare, with his vicious teeth exposed, caused the man to scream in terror. The captain's men quickly pulled him to safety. Socrates was steaming with anger. He slowly withdrew, but the captain could not help but notice from Socrates' stare that this had not been an accident.

Socrates stayed next to the sunken vessel for the next three days, sobbing over the loss of his sister. They had been constant companions and shared an obsessive love for their Aegean home; however, the water had become progressively polluted, and as fish, they had no way of knowing if any humans even cared, let alone had any plans of reversing the danger to the water that the pollution was causing. Socrates was now also noticing that the baitfish populations had become so sparse from anglers overfishing the bait schools that food sources for the resident fish were nearly exhausted. He felt he had no choice but to leave his home. He was not going to become another dead statistic. One way or another, he was going to try to honor his dead sister's memory with an attempt at finding solutions to the problems fish were facing in their vast watery world. For now, he had to get away. He had no real plan, and he did not know where he would end up, but he knew he could not stay there and allow the loss of his sister to haunt him. He took a moment to look around one last time then turned and swam away.

Chapter Two

As Socrates entered the area where the Aegean and Mediterranean seas merge, he noticed that food was scarce there, too. Only three days into his trip, he was desperately hungry. He was trying to keep away from the shoreline. The water near the shore seemed to have very little oxygen and was virtually devoid of sea life. It seemed as though most of the fish, both large and small, stayed closer to the center of the sea, the deepest part—just the opposite of how things used to be.

Seemingly out of nowhere, a tightly serried school of herring darted by. Without even thinking, Socrates blasted through the middle of the school, opened his mouth, seized three of the delicious little fish, and gulped them down ravenously. Suddenly, large fish began appearing from every direction and clobbering the school of herring. Fish parts were floating everywhere, and Socrates took immediate advantage of the situation by eating the bits of leftover fish as quickly as he could. When the herring school suddenly disappeared, Socrates went into hiding; the large fish looked as though they were still hungry, and he did not want to be on the dinner menu—however, he had not escaped their notice.

"Where did he go?" called out a roaming shark. "I know he's here! I saw him swimming for this rock pile after the baitfish disappeared! He should not be too hard to find. He's pretty big!"

Socrates was frightened. Nevertheless, he was also powerful and smart. He had settled into a large depression in a rock pile and was waiting for just the right moment to fight his way out of this. The moment arrived quickly. He took advantage of his strategic hiding place and ambushed the unsuspecting shark as it swam by; he bolted out and bit down hard on the back of one of the shark's anterior fins. Socrates' teeth ripped the flesh open; the shark panicked and grimaced in pain as the other sharks now turned toward the smell of new blood in the water. Socrates hurried back to the shelter of his hiding place, leaving the shark that he had attacked as the now hunted. As the large predators chased their victim, Socrates heard voices coming from the murky water.

"Did you see that? I have never seen anything like it. Who is that?"

"I don't know," came another voice. "But he sure seems to know what he's doing. Where do you think he came from?"

Socrates realized that they were talking about him.

"Wherever it is, I don't think I would want to visit there. Not unless he was my friend and wanted to go along."

"Ditto on that, dude."

Socrates could not see who was talking. He called out in the general direction of the phantom voices. "I don't know who you are, but come out *now!*"

In an instant, about fifty rockfish were front and center, facing Socrates. All of them looked scared out of their wits.

"I'm not your enemy!" Socrates blurted, heart still racing from the confrontation with the shark. "I am not from around here, but I am definitely not your enemy. So lighten up! Okay?"

"Got it," came back a single, mumbled reply. Socrates noticed the voice coming from an odd-looking fish that resembled a perch. "It's just that we've never seen anyone take on a shark before. You have to admit, it is a bit unusual. You don't do this kind of thing every day, do you?"

"You've got no idea of the horrors I've had to face. The shark ranks right up there on my prefer-not-to-do list, but I have learned that you have to face your fears. You can't do that by backing down every time you face a dangerous situation!"

The rockfish were looking back and forth at each other, obviously uninterested in what Socrates was saying. They definitely did not have the courage he possessed. All they could think about was going back into hiding. Socrates detected their cowardice and was disappointed at their lack of fortitude; however, everything in the Mediterranean Sea seemed a bit off-kilter. He then very kindly ended the conversation. "I am sorry to have frightened you. You can go back to your hiding places now."

The fish all scrambled away in an instant. Socrates shook his head and continued his trek west, eager to escape an ocean even more disappointing than the one he had first left. As he periodically took time to rest, he would contemplate his ultimate goal. He wanted to end up in a nice, warm ocean with clean water and many good friends, but this goal seemed more like an impossible dream—however, he felt that dreams were not necessarily beyond the grasp of those willing to take the risks involved in making them happen. Moreover, he was determined to work hard to make this dream a reality. For now, though, he would have to remain on constant alert for whatever danger he would have to face next.

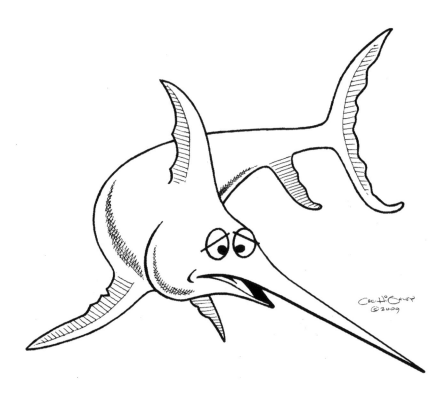

POKER

Chapter Three

For the next several weeks, Socrates pushed forward. Food was scarce, and the ocean currents were still quite cold. However, he was finally able to escape the Mediterranean Sea through a conspicuous, narrow channel. He was now entering the majestic Atlantic Ocean, seeking warmer currents by moving south. Moreover, the sea life seemed to be getting more abundant. Then, one day, out of nowhere, a large shadow engulfed Socrates, frightening him. Looking up, he recognized the familiar sight of a fishing boat. It was moving slowly with long lines and hooks baited with dead squid. Huge swordfish started appearing out of the deep and viciously attacking the lines.

"No!" Socrates yelled. "It's a trap!"

But none of them listened. The swordfish were so hungry that they gulped the bait without any examination. Magnificent battles ensued, and the swordfish kept disappearing from the water and onto the boat. To Socrates, this did not seem to be the natural order of things. He felt sad that some two hundred of the swordfish had disappeared from their ocean home.

Then something hit Socrates—*hard*.

"*Owww!*"

Socrates was in pain and frightened. He spun around to see what had jabbed him from behind; there was a strange-looking swordfish just hovering there and staring at him. Socrates took a defensive posture, anticipating another fight. However, the swordfish asked him, "*What?*"

"What do you mean 'what'? You almost skewered me!" Socrates exclaimed.

The swordfish replied, "Hey, who are you guys? I don't recognize you."

Socrates was curious about what the swordfish meant by 'you guys.' He slowly looked around; perhaps there was someone behind him? No, there was only him. Looking closer at the swordfish, Socrates noticed that he seemed to be staring at his nose.

Socrates curiously asked, "Who are you, and why are you staring at your nose?"

"My name is Poker, and this is *not* a nose—it's a sword. I am a *swordfish*, and the only one in the Atlantic with *two* swords, for your information. I am not staring at my swords; I am staring at *you* two. By the way, your choreography is great. You move in perfect rhythm, and even your lip movements match when you talk. That is so awesome."

Socrates was a bit confused. He once again looked around as though there was some phantom fish playing a trick on him or something, but no, he was the only one there besides this strange-looking, cross-eyed swordfish. Socrates realized that this fish had a problem and kindly replied, "Uh, thanks, I guess. Poker, is it? So why do they call you Poker?"

"Well, my swords are a little sharper than normal, and, unfortunately, I have had quite a few similar accidents running into the backs of other fish." Socrates started to laugh but realized that Poker had real issues. Therefore, he asked, "Have your eyes always been crossed, or do you remember a time when you saw things differently?"

"Well," began Poker, "now that you mention it, one day when my friends and I were in a feeding frenzy, I rammed my head into one of those boats. Since then, everyone I see seems to have an identical twin."

Socrates approached Poker. "Have you been able to eat much lately? Because you do not look quite as strong as all the fish, I saw you with earlier. By the way, where are they?"

Poker hung his head. "They always leave me by myself. It's as though they're embarrassed to be around me. And no—I haven't eaten in days."

Socrates felt sorry for Poker. Suddenly, he had an idea. "Poker, my name is Socrates. I could be your friend. And maybe we can help each other."

"You're willing to hang out with me?"

"Absolutely; after all, I have no one, either. And with your sword—which is awesome, by the way—and my skill at finding schools of fish, we could be a great team."

Poker was so excited. He had not had a real friend since the day he had rammed his head into the bottom of that fishing boat.

"There's just one thing," said Socrates. "There are not two of me—just one. I think we ought to get busy trying to fix your eye problem. Hmm …"

Socrates thought long and hard while they swam slowly along. After about an hour, he got an idea.

"Say, you claimed your eyes went crossed when you hit your head on the bottom of a boat, right? Well, you must have had your head turned to the side when you hit it; otherwise, you would have hit the boat with your sword."

Poker blinked. "Now that you mention it, I *was* sore over my right eye for a few days."

"Would you be willing to try something to correct your eyes, even if it really hurt?"

Poker nodded. "I'll do whatever it takes. But promise me one thing."

"What's that?"

"Promise me that no matter what happens, you won't abandon me. I don't think I can endure any more isolation."

"On my life—I promise," vowed Socrates. "From now on, we are best friends."

Poker's somber expression quickly turned into an anxious and excited one. Then, in a burst of power, he exclaimed,

"Let's *do* this thing!" Then he blinked his crossed eyes rapidly for a moment, looking confused. "By the way, what is it we're doing?"

"You'll see—at least, *hopefully* you'll see."

They both started laughing.

"Oh, that's good," replied Poker. "Now I have a friend who just happens to be a comedian."

"C'mon, let's get going," chuckled Socrates. "We've got work to do."

"What do I do?" asked Poker.

"Just listen; listen for the sound of a boat."

As they were busy searching out a boat, Poker suddenly realized something.

"So—does this mean that I only have *one* sword?"

Socrates looked hesitant. "Um, that would be correct."

"Oh, man—this is bad. This is *bad*! I have been bragging for months about my *two* swords! Everyone in the ocean must think I am the biggest idiot anyone has ever seen! No *wonder* they turn away from me, snickering and not taking me seriously. Another swordfish challenged me to a duel one day, and I explained to him that the odds of two swords against one were not fair. He gave me an odd look, shrugged, and swam away. Oh, man—I can't believe how big of a doofus I've been!"

Socrates tried hard to contain his laughter. His eyes were swelling and his lips were quivering. "Well, there is one thing about it, my friend," he finally managed. "It just goes to show ya."

"Show me what?"

"It's just a saying."

"It's just a saying about what?"

"Oh, it's about nothing in particular. You know; it's what you say when you're at a loss for words."

"Thanks, buddy. That's really helpful," Poker said sarcastically. He kept mumbling the words to himself for some time, but then he caught on to the ridiculous phrase and started snickering. Socrates was already laughing so hard from listening to Poker's mumbling about it that he had a hard time concentrating on what they needed to do to fix Poker's problem. This was absolutely the funniest situation he had ever experienced.

The two continued swimming southward until they suddenly felt the water temperature becoming warmer. Socrates commented on it.

"It's the current," said Poker. "This is a warm current. Where there is a warm current, there are usually fish. And where there are fish—"

In unison, they said, "—there are boats!"

Almost instantly, baitfish appeared from every direction. Poker was so hungry that he started to chase the tiny fish. However, Socrates reprimanded him.

"Poker! Stop! *Focus!*"

"Oh, that's good," replied Poker. "That's real nice: I'm *cross-eyed,* and I'm supposed to focus."

Again, they laughed, but Socrates quickly reminded him, "We have to concentrate here!"

Suddenly, the swordfish perked up. "Hear that?" he asked.

"Yes!" replied Socrates. "It's a boat. Are you ready, Poker?"

"As ready as I'll ever be! By the way—what am I ready for?"

Socrates was starting to think that there was more wrong with Poker than just his eyesight; however, being a true friend, he laid out his plan in detail. Poker's response was halfway expected.

"I'm supposed to do *what*? Ram the *other* side of my head into that boat? Are you *crazy*?"

"Well, think about it," said Socrates. "If hitting your head on the right side made your eyes go bad, maybe hitting your head on the left side will straighten them out."

"Or maybe I'll see *four* of you instead of two! Did you stop to consider *that*?"

Socrates had suspected Poker would wimp out, so he swam in front of him, careful of his friend's sharp point. "Poker, you said you'd try! Are you going to wimp out of this?"

Those were fighting words. "I'm *no* wimp! Got that?" Poker growled.

Socrates remained calm. "Then let's try this and see if it works. Just think: you will go down in history as the only swordfish that took on a boat—*twice*. Even if the first time was an accident, and *this* time is an attempt to remedy the consequences, who needs to know? All the fish will just think that you, Poker, are the toughest swordfish in the ocean. Why, you will be famous. As for *me*, well, let us just say that the truth is safe with me. Let others think what they want."

Poker was suddenly feeling a surge of toughness he had never felt before. The idea of being the toughest swordfish in the ocean had gotten his adrenaline pumping. He was speeding around, darting back and forth, and building up his courage.

"That's it," coached Socrates, "Get mad! A boat like *this* got you into this mess to start with! Are you going to let them get away with it? How many of your friends did they take with their lines the last time—one hundred? *Two* hundred? You *know* they will never stop until they take you, too! Show those jerks that Poker is no one to mess with!"

In an absolute rage, Poker charged. The boat rocked hard to one side. The deckhands were shocked at the impact; they all rushed to the side and looked over the rail to see what had happened. Socrates himself was amazed at how quickly and fiercely Poker had attacked the boat. Seeing a large group of swordfish nearby that had frozen upon witnessing Poker's vicious attack, Socrates stuck his head out of the water and yelled, "And don't bring that boat back in these waters again, or Poker will *sink* you next time!"

Amazingly, the boat began to move away. All of the swordfish were awestruck at the bravery of Poker and Socrates. Socrates strutted a little, soaking up the admiration. He turned to high-five Poker but did not see him; Socrates looked around and saw his friend's limp body sinking slowly toward the ocean floor.

"No!" Socrates cried out, "Nooo!"

He was rushing down to help when he saw a huge shark appear out of the depths, heading straight for Poker. Socrates was only a cod but a tough one, with rows of sharp teeth gracing his big, strong jaws. Without even thinking, he darted toward the back of the shark, opened his large jaws, and sunk his teeth into its head.

The shark screamed in agony. Shaking its head violently, the shark tried to free itself from the attack. Socrates held on. *Not today, big guy, not today*, Socrates thought. *That is my friend, and he has been hurt enough.*

Suddenly, the shark screamed again. Poker had come to and, in a burst of speed, rammed his sword into the shark's backside.

"They don't call me 'Poker' for nothing!" he yelled gleefully.

The shark's eyes had opened to about five times their normal size. Socrates still had his teeth in the shark's head. Now his eyes were staring in the shark's eyes, with only about two inches separating them.

"Let me go!" screamed the shark. "Let me go!"

Poker swam alongside the shark and, with a scowl, stated, "Tell all your friends about this. Let them know that if they decide to mess with a cod or a swordfish again, we will come for them! Got it?"

"Got it! Now let me go!" pleaded the shark.

"Okay, Socrates, let him go."

However, Socrates was not finished. He slowly removed his jaws and teeth from his victim's head, looked the shark in the eyes with a mean stare, and yelled, "Boo!"

The shark screamed and swam away in panic.

Socrates and Poker just looked at each other in silence for a moment. Then Socrates shrugged and said, "Hey, what are friends for?"

After a few quiet seconds, they suddenly burst into uncontrollable laughter.

"Did you *see* how big that shark's eyes got?" laughed Poker.

"I did," choked Socrates. "He was trying to look upward, backward, and sideways. He completely freaked out. When you rammed him, his eyes went crossed like *yours* before you hit the boat, but about five times larger. Then when I said "Boo," did you see that little present he left in the water as he swam away? Now *that* was funny. It is absolutely the first time I ever saw a shark scared enough to do that. And the bubbles—did you notice the bubbles? When was the last time you saw a shark do *bubbles*? We actually *scared the bubbles* out of him."

"You're the man!" yelled Poker. "You're the man!"

"Hey, you ram your head into a boat and then skewer a shark, and you call *me* the man? *You're* the man!"

"Hey," replied Poker. "Together … *we* the man!"

The other swordfish were curious about these two extraordinarily different fish. How had they learned to work so well together as a team? In addition, their antics were hilarious. One of the swordfish cautiously swam toward them and asked, "You guys hungry? We know where there's a *huge* amount of herring, and we would be honored to have you two join us."

Socrates and Poker were still laughing, but they did have a gnawing hunger in their stomachs. They turned to the swordfish, and Socrates replied, "We'd be happy to. Lead the way." Poker quickly added, "But do *not* follow the shark—he's got a little problem!"

Again, the two exploded in laughter.

Chapter Four

That afternoon proved the best day that either Socrates or Poker had experienced in a long time. They spent most of their time laughing hysterically and recounting their experience with the boat and the shark. The school of swordfish had guided them to the largest feast of herring they had seen in years. Their hunger had been so extreme that they had gorged themselves. The whole feeding frenzy had been pure mayhem; Socrates thought back to Poker's experience of running into a boat the first time and could now understand how that kind of accident could happen if a boat showed up in the middle of such an event. However, today there was no boat, just fish; it was wonderful. When the feeding was over, Socrates looked like a cross between a cod and a blowfish. Everyone lazily meandered along; there was no hurry now to find food. For a couple of weeks, they enjoyed cruising northwest across the Atlantic Ocean, sharing stories of all their adventures and the wonders they had seen.

A full two weeks into their peaceful journey, however, everything started to change. The swells on the open ocean began to rise. The wind was blowing hard. Socrates now came face-to-face with a serious dilemma: he was a cod and was not used to the violent, open Atlantic Ocean. Detecting his concern, the swordfish turned toward a well-known ocean trench with huge walls that would provide Socrates protection. Their respect for Socrates was becoming obvious. They had no need of finding shelter themselves, but they knew Socrates would never survive the journey across the Atlantic in this massive storm. Moreover, even though Socrates knew what was happening, no one uttered a word about this situation; the swordfish just quietly formed a circle around him and slowly guided him through the deep trench while they waited out the storm.

On the second day of the storm, in a private conversation, Poker asked Socrates what kind of cod he was.

"What do you mean, 'what kind'? I'm a cod."

"C'mon," pushed Poker. "Everyone knows there are different kinds of cod. Like Atlantic cod, True cod, Ling cod, Tomcod. You know—different kinds."

"Yep, that's me," Socrates replied.

"Which one are you?"

"I'm the 'different kind' of cod."

Poker thought about it for a few seconds, looked at Socrates quizzically, and then laughed. "*You,* my friend, are a 'DK' cod. Do you get it? You *are* a 'different kind.' Do you see how tough that sounds? If anyone asks, just say, in a deep voice, 'I'm a DK cod.' You have to look a bit defiant when you say it, but not necessarily all-out *threatening*."

"Wow, that's not bad, Poker. Maybe that last confrontation with the boat corrected more than your eyesight. Thanks, pal."

Poker did not quite know how to take the last boat reference, so he just dismissed it. He added, "And the name is our secret. No one will ever know what 'DK' really stands for."

They both looked at each other with that look that friends give each other when a secret is sealed. Socrates went over and over the name in his mind, even practicing aloud to get the hang of saying it. "I'm a DK cod," he asserted repeatedly to no one in particular. He finally gave up when he realized that it was unlikely that anyone besides Poker would actually ask him what kind of cod he was. However, little did he know that Poker was already spreading the word of Socrates' legacy among the other swordfish, telling them that Socrates was from the terrifying 'DK cod' species—and word spreads amazingly fast in the ocean.

BILLY BLUE   AUNT DOROTHY

Chapter Five

It took three full days for the storm to abate and another two weeks to complete their journey across the Atlantic. Even though they had eaten frequently, the stress of the distance traveled demanded as much food as they could possibly find. Now, however, not having eaten for the last two days, their pangs of hunger were kicking in.

"Not to worry," stated one of the swordfish. "I've got a pretty good idea about what we can expect just up ahead."

The water was getting shallower; they were approaching a huge landmass. Socrates was apprehensive. This place was all new to him, and a tinge of fear often comes with things that are not familiar. However, he peeled off from the group to check out a large bay. Suddenly, he was startled by a voice.

"Hey! Whatcha doin' in our neighborhood?" asked a strange, sleek fish. He rolled his lip back to reveal top and bottom rows of perfect, razor-sharp teeth. "We don't take too kindly to strangers, you know, and you look like someone who's not from around here. This can be a dangerous place, and if you want to avoid trouble, maybe you should just turn around and leave—or else my friends and I will have to escort you out of here, which may not be so healthy for you!"

Out of nowhere, three other fish appeared. All of them had scars, presumably from some narrow escapes with larger predator fish. One had obviously had his lip ripped out by a fishing hook. They all appeared menacing and aching for a fight. Socrates remained calm and replied, "No problem. Your neighborhood looked interesting, and I am only traveling through. I do not need an escort. I'll be on my way."

"Hey, did you hear that? This intruder is going to leave. I think he might be going to run home to his mama. Is this neighborhood too tough for you?" The bluefish all started laughing and surrounded Socrates. However, just then, a powerful voice penetrated the circle from out of the dim background.

"I hope you boys know what you're doing," it said challengingly.

"Who is that? Where is that voice coming from?"

The bluefish were obviously nervous; slowly moving into view was none other than Poker. He smiled and said, "This ought to be good. I don't think any fewer than thirty blues have ever taken on a DK cod and lived to tell about it."

The blues immediately cowered in fear. "You're a *DK* cod?" the first one, their leader, asked. They all started trembling.

Socrates nodded with a sly smile. "Yes, I'm a DK cod. And I'm trespassing in your waters, you were saying?"

The blue leader began stammering. "H-hey, n-not a problem! What I said b-before, forget about it. N-no hard feelings, right?" He cleared his throat and regained some composure. "You know, we've heard about you DKs, and we are, um, *pleased* to have you visit our neighborhood. My name is Billy—Billy Blue. These are my cousins Vinny, Georgie, and Tony. Hurry, Vinny, get our guests some bunker fish. They look hungry, and *you* could be on the menu—if you know what I mean."

Vinny, Georgie, and Tony all bolted in fear. Socrates and Poker decided, without saying a word, to play this out. They kept their faces stern as they stared down Billy.

"Hey, why not let me show you around?" he offered. "A little hospitality never hurt no one, right?"

Socrates and Poker agreed to accompany Billy but kept up their defiant- and dangerous-looking appearances. They both knew the advantage of disarming opponents with a scare tactic.

"This is where my world happens," stated Billy. "Uh, we don't go anywhere, 'cause, hey—where else is there to go? We got it all here: fresh eels, fresh bunker ... You know, only the best."

Socrates whispered to Poker. "You ever heard of those fish?"

"No, but I'm not in the mood to be picky right now. I'm hungry."

"Gotcha," said Socrates.

Vinny, Georgie, and Tony all returned in a flash, their mouths stuffed with bunker fish and eels. Once the blues released the fish, Poker and Socrates snapped them up with lightning speed. They had learned—through hard experience in rough, open ocean water—not to hesitate when it came to food. Billy Blue and his companions, who thought their own feeding prowess to be legendary, realized they were no match for a DK cod or a swordfish.

Billy Blue approached Socrates and Poker, when he was sure they had finished eating, and, in a very humble tone, offered to get them more food.

"No, we're fine," replied Socrates. "We could use a little rest, though. We've been on the move for a long time."

"We've got the perfect place," smiled Billy. "Follow me, and see how Jersey blues treat their honored guests." The blues started moving quickly in one direction.

"Where do you think they're taking us?" whispered Poker.

Socrates shrugged and said, also whispering, "I don't think we'll have to worry about it too much. After all, he *did* state that we are honored guests."

"Maybe so," said Poker. "But don't let your guard down. You never know; you could end up cross-eyed."

"Or doing bubbles," quipped Socrates.

They both tried hard not to burst out laughing but did give into some snickering. All of a sudden, Poker got a seriously sour look on his face and then belched quite loudly.

"Ah, buddy!" said Socrates. "What is your problem? Your breath *stinks*!"

Poker looked at him and asked, "Did you eat any of those eels?"

Socrates shook his head. "I was careful to leave those for you. They did not really look that appealing and had a terrible smell. Even as hungry as I was, there was no way I was going to bite into one of those. As a matter of fact, I was surprised to see *you* picking them off."

"Thanks, pal," Poker replied with a sneer. "I've got to start examining my food more closely before I inhale it." Then he belched loudly again and moaned. "The taste in my mouth is awful! What am I going to do?"

The Bluefish had moved a significant distance away from Poker because they had smelled it, too; Billy called over and explained. "It's not infrequent that the breath goes bad after eating the eels—especially when we get them from near the pipes."

"What pipes?" asked Socrates.

"Not now," replied Billy. "Tomorrow, we'll show you. Tonight, though, we have to do something to take care of your friend's breath. Vinny, go to Aunt Dorothy's rock pile and ask her what to do for eel breath. Make it quick! My eyes are starting to burn!"

It was obvious why Billy had chosen Vinny for the task: he was fast. It did not take ten minutes for him to return with claws apparently bitten off a huge lobster.

"Chew this," instructed Vinny. "Chew it good. The meat is sweet, and the shell helps clean the mouth. Aunt Dorothy says it's a sure thing for your problem."

Poker immediately followed directions and chewed the sweet morsels with delight.

"This is probably the best thing I've eaten in my entire life," he swooned.

He kept on chewing and savoring the tasty morsels. His eyes were rolling in his head over the sweet flavor. When he finished swallowing, his breath was fresh, and his indigestion was gone.

"That's the only thing I ever want to eat again!" blurted out Poker. "What *was* that?"

Billy laughed. "That'll only happen in your dreams. Aunt Dorothy was generous, but she does have her limits—aside from the fact that those lobsters are getting scarce. They used to be everywhere, but since the water is changing, the good ones are not so common anymore."

Socrates was starting to feel a sickening dread. He realized what was happening here: the water pollution was bad. It resembled the pollution in the Aegean and Mediterranean seas. However, this day was well along, and he and Poker needed some rest. Billy arranged for them to stay close to Aunt Dorothy's place, since the water was cleaner and more refreshing there.

Chapter Six

The following day began with Socrates anxiously swimming back and forth near a freshwater inlet to the bay. Hundreds of fish were swarming around the area, preparing for their daily feeding activities, when Poker shouted out: "Hey, Socrates, what's happening?"

Every fish in the area froze in pure shock, especially Billy and his cousins.

"Wait a minute!" chimed Billy. "You're not *the* Socrates, the one that took on a shark, are you?"

"That would be correct," replied Poker. "He is the one and only. You should have heard that shark scream!"

"But you didn't say *nothin'* yesterday."

"Like what?" asked Socrates?

"Like your *name*," Billy responded in a quivering tone. "You're, like, the most famous fish in the ocean. And you, you're *Poker*, the swordfish that took on the boat and almost sank it—then turned around, half dead, and rammed a shark!"

Poker thought that sounded good, so he looked at Billy and agreed, saying, "Yep, that's about the size of it."

Word spread instantly throughout the bay about the identity of the newcomers. Fish, by the *hundreds*, started swarming Socrates and Poker to hear them tell of their travels. The entire morning was lost as Poker embellished their tales of adventure. Then, when everyone's hunger kicked in, there was a quick departure. Billy, however, invited Poker and Socrates to dine at Aunt Dorothy's place.

"When I tell her who you are, she'll understand."

And understand she did. She had previously heard, in detail, the events surrounding the growing legacy of Socrates and Poker. She immediately snatched four big lobsters out of the rocks and gave them to her guests. *Now* Socrates understood what Poker had been talking about the day before; these lobsters were sumptuous. They thanked Aunt Dorothy multiple times and then settled in for some serious conversation. Socrates, in a very concerned tone, began.

"Aunt Dorothy, what's happening to the water around here?"

"Oh, Socrates, it's awful. Everything used to be so beautiful and clean. Now, almost every inlet to the bay stinks with filth and sewage. The fish that live in the rivers have told us about areas where horrible-smelling sludge is flowing directly into the rivers, and it all makes its way into our bay. Sometimes we have to swim *miles* out to sea to get a break from the stench. One account from years past described a time when one of the rivers actually caught fire and burned for days. Now, even though it appears as though some of the bad water entering the bay from rivers is showing some improvement, there are still horrible places. Fish are developing deformities, and the shellfish in those areas are pure poison to eat. However, the inlet where I reside is clean and has proven to be an isolated haven for those fortunate enough to find it; the only problem is that there is no way it can sustain every fish in the region."

"Would you mind showing us some of the worst areas?" asked Socrates.

"No, I wouldn't mind at all. But I will warn you that what you're going to see will probably make you sick."

The first area they examined was that of the pipes that Billy Blue had mentioned the day before. It was sickening; Socrates watched raw, stinking, filthy water with huge chunks of sludge flowing directly into the bay through underwater pipes. The eels did not seem to mind as they hung in the current and actually fed on some of the chunky sludge. Vinny, Georgie, and Tony grew frightened when Poker gave them a scowling stare; this was the place where they had rounded up the eels that he had eaten the day before. Then, everyone watched in horror as a big catfish wandered into the bay from a nearby river and started heaving violently. It coughed up a huge, stinky bait ball.

"Aw, that's enough!" shrieked Poker. "I'm out of here!"

As he turned to leave, a tiny voice came out of the rocks: "I see you."

Poker noticed a lobster in the rocks with his back to everyone.

"You see *who*?" asked Poker. "What—do you have eyes in the back of your head?"

"Only one!" exclaimed Aunt Dorothy.

Poker and Socrates, with raised eyebrows, turned and stared at Aunt Dorothy and asked, in perfect unison, "He's got only one *what*?"

"He has only one eye in the back of his head. He still has two in the front."

Socrates now started noticing that this place was nothing more than a slum of stench and deformed sea life. As they continued on their tour of the bay, they happened upon a shocking scene only about a mile from the pipes. They saw an eerie greenish, glowing, oozing mass seeping from a small pipe. On top of the pipe were some neatly stacked rocks that nearly entirely hid it from view. The water in the area not only had a strange smell but also was bitter.

"Socrates! Get back!" screamed Aunt Dorothy. "You're too close!"

Socrates quickly withdrew, but it was too late. He started coughing and sputtering. His body lurched and jerked violently.

"What *is* that? Ugh! Help me! I can't breathe!"

"Quick!" cried Aunt Dorothy. "Everyone help him, and follow me!"

The bluefish and Poker hurried Socrates out into the open ocean.

"Keep him moving!" shouted Aunt Dorothy. "Don't let him stop! Open your mouth, Socrates! Make yourself open your mouth!" Socrates struggled to respond. He was near to being choked into unconsciousness and was forcing himself to follow Aunt Dorothy's commands. After almost two hours, Socrates started to recover; the refreshing salt water had finally balanced the effect of the poisoned water. Aunt Dorothy was crying hysterically because she had failed to warn him of the danger of getting too close to that particular source of pollution.

"Auntie," coughed Socrates, "I'm okay. I am going to be okay. I should have waited and followed you instead of racing ahead. My curiosity got the best of me. Trust me; I am okay. It won't happen again."

Socrates then very gently rubbed his face against hers to console her.

"Thank you, Auntie," Socrates continued, "for responding so quickly. It is no wonder why everyone around here loves you. You're amazing."

Socrates' gentleness and encouragement helped Aunt Dorothy regain her composure. Then she began to sob again. "That's another example of the horror that we're dealing with!"

Socrates was appalled and angry. The pollution here was terrible. He thought back to the problems of his home in the Aegean Sea, which were admittedly much less acute than these were. The other water inlets they examined that day were not as bad as the pipes or the green-poison outlet, but the oxygen level was definitely too low for most underwater life. Even more importantly, underwater plants were being killed off by the pollution, which was also affecting the oxygen level of the water.

Finally, they decided to return to Aunt Dorothy's place. For the rest of the afternoon, Socrates carefully listened to her assessment of their problems. Then, together, they rounded up the leaders of entire schools of fish and came up with a strategic plan of action. There was no way Socrates was going to let the polluters get away with the destruction they were causing to the fish habitat.

Chapter Seven

First on the agenda was to make sure all the local fish schools moved nightly through Aunt Dorothy's freshwater inlet in two-hour intervals. This would help raise the oxygen levels in their bodies before moving back out into the bay. In addition, they decided to herd all the eels away from the pipes to other inlets where the water was better. When they no longer stunk, the fish in the bay could eat them. Vinny was given the privilege of overseeing that job. The orders came directly from Poker, who still wore a scowl each time he looked at Vinny.

Next, Socrates engaged Billy Blue in a private conversation. "Billy, who do you feel is the bravest and craziest fish in these waters?"

Billy thought hard for a few minutes. This was not an easy question to answer, considering the location of the bay. Everyone here was a bit half-baked. However, after some careful thought, a smile crept over his face.

"You want someone brave and crazy, huh?" he said with satisfaction. "That would have to be Leo the dogfish. It is a bit questionable if he is actually brave or just not too bright, but he *has* done some crazy stuff—like one time, he waited until one of those little fishing boats came to a stop in the bay. He was curious about the propeller, you know, how it turns around and around so fast. Well, Leo decided to wrap his mouth over it and wait until it started up again. It was *not* a brilliant thing to do. When the engine started up, Leo looked like a waterspout. The boat was not moving, because the blades could not push any water. When the person on the boat shut the engine off and lifted the little motor out of the water, there hung Leo, with his eyes all scrambled in his head. The person on the boat pried Leo's mouth off the propeller and tossed him back in the water—followed by a few choice words, if you know what I mean. Leo swam in circles for *days* after that. He kept trying to say something that no one could understand. You know, with his mouth so mangled and all. The other fish were thinking he was trying to warn them not to try putting their mouth over a propeller. He kept saying something like, 'Ah eww! Ah eww!' No one could figure it out until the cuts on his mouth started healing. Finally, his speech started making sense: he was saying 'yahoo!' To this day, he says it was the most fun thing he has ever done, even though there was significant damage to his mouth. He's the guy everyone takes bets on when there's a weird challenge or something."

Socrates could not help laughing, but Leo sounded exactly like the fish he was looking for.

"Do you know where he hangs out?" Socrates asked Billy.

"Oh, yeah, I know—*everyone* knows where to find Leo. He hangs out under the docks by the big bridge. His feeding prowess is definitely not as efficient as what it used to be, so he waits for people to throw their food into the water. It makes it easy for him."

"Let's go talk to him. I've got something in mind that he'll probably be interested in."

The docks were some distance from where Socrates and Billy were. It took hours for them to get there. When they arrived, it was not hard to spot Leo. He had scars around his mouth and teeth that seemed to go in every direction. He was munching on some strange-looking food. People up above seemed amused by Leo feeding on whatever they would throw him.

"Leo, my friend!" called Billy. "It's me, Billy. Billy Blue. I have someone here who wants to meet the bravest fish in these parts. So hey, I'm thinking, who else could that be but my old friend Leo? Besides, all the blues have been wondering how you're getting along. You got a minute?"

Leo was excited to hear Billy's voice. "Wow, Billy, you've come to see me? That is so awesome! So what has been happening in your end of the bay? I really miss seeing all of you. How is everyone? It has been a while."

Billy smiled at Leo's reaction to his presence. "Everyone's good. Like you, we're all just trying to make it from day to day. Say—I brought along a friend who needs some help. He needs specialized skills and someone who is, you know, *fearless*. I immediately thought of you. Would you mind hearing him out?"

"No problem. I'll do anything for an old friend. However, I have given up on propellers. It was fun once, but I've definitely changed some of my youthful behavior."

Socrates and Billy chuckled. They were thinking of what Leo's incident with the propeller must have looked like underwater.

"So, who *is* your friend anyway?"

"Leo, meet Socrates. Socrates, this is Leo."

"Not *the* Socrates?"

"One and the same," replied Billy.

Socrates moved forward in greeting. "I'm pleased to meet you, Leo. Billy has told me about how courageous you are.

And I must say that I'm impressed." Leo beamed upon hearing these words coming from the individual he recognized as the toughest fish in the ocean.

"What do you have in mind? How can I assist you?" asked Leo, in a tough Jersey tone.

"How familiar are you with the area of the pipes where Billy lives?" Socrates asked him.

"That place is terrible. It drives me crazy to hear about how bad things have gotten there. I often wonder if there is anything we can do to stop it."

"I've got an idea, if you're interested. Maybe we can send a message that will get someone's attention. It will be risky, and once we start, there will not be any turning back. So, what do you say? Are you up for a challenge?"

"Let's do it!" said Leo emphatically. "I've been waiting for a challenge like this for a long time. However, could you first tell me about the shark story? The part about the bubbles really cracks me up. After all, I'm a shark. I'm a small shark, but still a shark. The bubble thing does not happen frequently. That had to be one scared shark. You must have laughed yourself sick. I know I did when I first heard about it. A swordfish by the name of Jacko stopped through here not long ago and had us all in stitches."

Socrates smiled when he heard Jacko's name. He was the leader of a group of swordfish that he and Poker had met when crossing the Atlantic. Jacko and Poker were the biggest cutups in the ocean. Poker had one day asked Jacko, "What do you get when a scared shark swims over the area called the Grand Banks?" Jacko had shrugged and said, "I don't know." Poker replied: "A deposit." The two of them had laughed for hours. All those two had done during the short time they had spent together was laugh and tell jokes. As Socrates and Billy led Leo back to Aunt Dorothy's inlet, Socrates treated Leo to this joke and a storytelling session that had Leo half dead from laughing by the time they arrived at their destination.

Chapter Eight

It was approaching midnight when Socrates, Billy, and Leo arrived back at Aunt Dorothy's place. The schools of fish were following the prescribed plan, taking turns at taking nourishment provided by the fresh water. What a relief it was for Socrates to feel the soothing affect the water had on his powerful body. Leo had not felt anything like it in years, and he was also excited to reacquaint himself with Aunt Dorothy, who welcomed him back, seeing that the years had settled him down a bit. The following morning started with an abrupt command by Socrates to gather the leaders of the schools of fish. Poker, Billy, Vinny, Georgie, and Tony all shared in gathering everyone into one spot in the bay. Aunt Dorothy and Leo accompanied Socrates. Socrates then addressed the group.

"All of you are dealing with one of the worst problems of pollution anyone has ever heard of. Together, we have to do something about it. This is not going to be easy, and there is a level of danger involved. Anyone that does not want to be included in helping us can leave now; there will be no hard feelings. However, know this: if you do nothing about this problem, not one of you will live much longer. The problem is *that* bad. I am sure that none of you wants to live like the cowardly fish I met some time ago in the Mediterranean Sea. They were scared of their own shadow. All they wanted to do was go into hiding. Are you like them, or are you going to prove to the world what the fish in this bay are really made of? You are *protectors*! You do not take it when someone threatens your environment! Am I right? Tell me—*who are you?*"

Socrates had whipped his listeners into a fury. A deafening roar came in answer: "*We* are protectors!"

"What was that? I couldn't hear you!"

"We are protectors! We are protectors!"

"So, are you willing to take charge?"

"Yes!" they shouted. "We will take charge!"

Poker swam over to Socrates and whispered, "Uh, I think you have their attention, buddy."

Socrates then had Poker, Billy, and Leo organize everyone into four strategic groups. The first group's job was to use every means possible to plug any pipes dumping sewage into the bay. They ingeniously were able to impress some river beavers to join in on the escapade. Nightly, they would haul any debris they could find as far up the pipes as they could manage without succumbing to the stench. It was caustic and horrible, but their efforts paid off. It only took about a week for the pipes to start backing up, and the flow of rotten filth started belching out the opposite direction. One of the pipes actually ruptured well above its entrance to the bay and sent a geyser of sewage about thirty feet into the air. It definitely got someone's attention, as vehicles with red and blue flashing lights gathered around on the land above the pipes. In addition, divers were going into the water to inspect what had happened; they would always emerge from the water heaving in disgust.

The second group's job was quite different; theirs was to gather every bit of rope and tangled mess of fishing line they could find. This required a high level of safety for the fish, in order to avoid strangling by getting their gills caught in the lines. Once they had gathered a sufficient amount, Socrates ordered the team to begin its mission. On a selected night, in four teams and twenty to a team, they swam under the cover of darkness, in strategic areas of the bay where fishing boats moor, and sought out every vessel that they could possibly find. They looped the rope and fishing line to the boats' propellers and tied the lines together whenever the boats were in close proximity to each other. Socrates watched, in amazement, the efficiency of this group, which was composed mainly of bluefish. They were fast and powerful and completed the harnessing of the lines and pieces of rope to at least a hundred boats that night. By morning, all of the fish were eagerly anticipating the outcome of their efforts.

The boat engines started roaring to life, and the disaster began. The ropes and lines wound around the propellers when the boats shifted into gear. The boats that had the lines looped together around their propellers pulled into each other, and some of the propellers tore off those boats. Never had anyone present heard more screaming than on that day. Everyone was shaking their fists at one another and throwing things at each other as though the other people were to blame. All the deckhands and anglers were feverishly trying to figure out what was happening. Again, it did not take long for another kind of boat to show up; this special boat also had red and blue flashing lights. Socrates now seemed to think that this special craft had something to do with checking out the problems. This became evident as the fish saw a good number of men forcefully subdued by the crewmembers of this special boat. Later that day, Socrates noticed something that amazed him.

"Look at that, Poker; look at all that mess of rope and line piled on the dock. Look at how much there is. The pile is bigger than the dock itself! And those guys from the boat with the lights on it are mad."

"Where did all of this come from?" yelled the man in charge. "How could this much mess *possibly* have ended up in our bay—unless you jerks have been throwing it over the side for a long, long time? I am informing you right now that we are closing this bay to all fishing. If we find anything linking any of this back to any of your specific boats, we will forever revoke your license to operate your boat in this bay! Do you really think that you can dump all this garbage in the water without it someday catching up with you? That's pure stupidity!"

He then got back into his boat and barked at his men to check their own propeller before moving on. The man never stopped yelling all the way across the bay.

"Wow," smiled Socrates. "We certainly got his attention."

Turning to the bluefish, he said, "Now *that's* what I call a job well done! You are incredible! However, we are not finished. There's something even more dangerous we've got to address." Socrates ordered Poker to go find Leo. "Let's see if he's come up with an idea about how to handle the green poison."

Poker sped away and found Leo discussing the matter with Aunt Dorothy. He quickly notified Socrates of their location.

"So, you two, what do you think? Have you come up with any ideas?"

"Well, this is going to be a tough one," answered Leo. "The problem is getting anyone close enough to the danger zone to do anything."

"I understand the concern," replied Socrates. "But why do we have to get close at all? Let's bring those people with the lights on their boats to the dumpsite. They obviously have an interest in all of this."

"*Now* you're talking," chirped Leo. "And I have the perfect way. However, I need you and Poker to help convince some two thousand dogfish in this bay to follow my lead. They typically are not interested in anything I have to say, because of my frequent scrapes with danger."

"That's not a problem," responded Socrates. "Poker, round up the blues. We will use them to help in our convincing process." Poker smiled and sped off. He somehow knew what Socrates was thinking. Within about an hour, the previous group of bluefish was reenlisted. This time, however, their job was to intimidate the dogfish into helping with one more necessary mission. Per Leo's instructions, the bluefish started chiding the dogfish all throughout the bay: "You're nothing but a big bunch of sissies. Leo told us that none of you has any spine. You're not even real fish; you're a bunch of *bottom feeders*. You may look like sharks, but you're about as scary as a ratfish."

Words like this caused the dogfish to swarm in huge numbers, which indicated they were angry enough to attack their intimidators, who carried on with the taunting.

"That's it! Let's take this fight to our special place and see if you can live up to your cowardly nature. There's a lot of tasty garbage on the bottom that ought to satisfy your legendary gourmet appetites!"

The dogfish had heard enough. They were now starting to chase the bluefish. The bluefish, on cue from Socrates, led their pursuers right past the boat with the flashing lights and the angry skipper who had been yelling at the anglers. The skipper was shocked. There were thousands of bluefish and dogfish in the water.

"What is going on *now*?" asked the skipper. His deckhands could only shrug their shoulders; they had no clue. However, the skipper was definitely determined to find out. He ordered his men to follow the fish.

The bluefish played the chase out to perfection. They stayed just ahead of their pursuers, all the time making sure to stay on the top of the water. The skipper, too, kept up his chase. This was definitely the weirdest thing he had ever seen. The bluefish neared the stretch of poisoned water, where the whole area emitted a strange, green glow. Things had gotten worse. Socrates now sped up to the leaders and commanded them to escape the area, leading the dogfish out of the danger zone. The blues raced away in a heartbeat, with the dogfish still giving chase. They turned and dove deep to get out of sight of the boat. It was then that the skipper noticed the glowing green water. He yelled at his crew to stop the boat.

The skipper felt sickened by the sour smell and the nasty, green goo that was sticking to the hull of his boat. He ordered his men to get samples of the water, turned on his flashing lights, got on the radio, and ordered some other vessels to the site. Over the next few days, he ordered all manner of special tests run on the water. On the fourth day, a large land machine showed up in order to lift the rocks out of the way of the nasty pipe. The reaction of the men doing this work was one of total revulsion. It appeared to Socrates that now someone was going to have to take responsibility for creating such a nightmare.

Socrates had given so much of his attention to all of this that he had completely forgotten about the dogfish. However, Leo had handled that well. On the day of the chase, he had personally apologized for embarrassing them into a fight. The bluefish had also graciously offered their apologies. Then Poker had further defused their anger by explaining how important they were to the outworking of this strategic plan; without them, it would not have worked. The dogfish were now feeling good after this explanation of their necessary contribution, and they even offered to help with anything else that needed attention in the bay.

"That's perfect," exclaimed Socrates. "We do need help with our fourth group. Poker, round up our final group. Billy, you can help him."

This group was composed of young fish representing most of the fish species in the bay. They were very excited to be a part of all these accomplishments and were anxious to get started on their fact-finding mission. Daily, after their feeding sessions, the dogfish would be accompanying these young fish to any areas found to have problems; the job was to collect information and report it back to Leo and Aunt Dorothy, who were now in charge of problem solving. Billy and the bluefish would be responsible for bringing problem areas to the attention of the people on the boats with the flashing lights, regardless of the mayhem it would require—which was right up Billy's alley. After several weeks, everything was in place. All of this activity had all the fish excited about working together to help solve the problems in their bay. Socrates and Poker were happy that everything was going so well; however, they were now prepared to continue their journey south. Their good-byes were going to be hard. Nevertheless, the bay was already starting to show signs of improvement. It had improved so much that the fishing boats were reappearing on the water. Most of the pipes causing the pollution had been located, and Billy was in the process of making some special arrangements for those areas not yet receiving proper attention.

This was the perfect legitimate job for someone who prided himself on mischief.

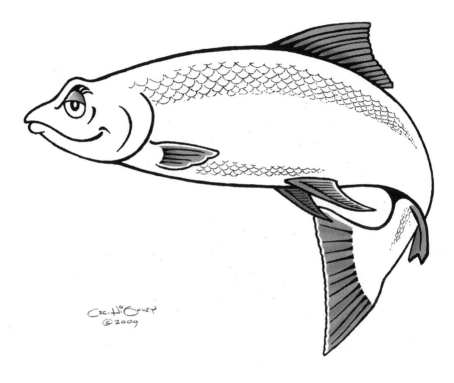

SLICK

Chapter Nine

"Are you sure you can't stay longer?" asked Aunt Dorothy, sobbing. She was now feeling as though Socrates was her own son. Socrates felt the same about her; she was his vision of the mother he had never known. Of all Socrates' good-byes in the bay, this one was the most difficult.

Suddenly, something interrupted them—a fish caught in what looked like a waterspout came swirling out of nowhere.

In addition, an almost deafening laughter was coming from all the fish in close proximity to the strange occurrence. This was eerie. The laughter was coming from places that Socrates could not make out due to poor visibility. Within a few moments, the event was over. All that was left of the phenomenon was a large, half-dead-looking salmon. Chuckles and laughter continued as voices rang out in the water. "Hey, Spinner, that was a nice show. We'll be by later, and you can humor us with another trick—or is that your only one? You're such a loser!"

The big salmon hung his head in obvious embarrassment. He did not even move; he was hoping that everyone else would finally peel away and go back to whatever else they had been doing. Socrates discerned that this fish needed some serious help. He called out, "Okay, now, the show's over! Everyone leave!"

At Socrates' command, all of the fish took off. The only ones who stayed were Aunt Dorothy, the blues, and Poker. Billy and the bluefish were still cracking up, and even Poker was snickering about what had gone on. Socrates motioned to Poker that they needed to talk privately.

"Poker," began Socrates in a low and obviously irritated tone of voice. "It seems to me there was a cross-eyed swordfish a while back that everyone laughed at. I often wonder how he felt when he heard people laugh." Poker slumped, feeling a surge of guilt. He got the point.

"Now," Socrates added, "Let's find out what's going on and see if there is something we can do for this guy!"

Aunt Dorothy was also one who had not found any humor in this event. She explained to Socrates what had happened.

"Some weeks ago, this salmon passed under a fishing boat and was snagged in the tail by a fishing lure. In a panic, he ran under the boat, and something sharp cut the line. As you can see, the lure is still in his tail, and he sometimes feverishly tries to get it out. There is no one who wants to help him. Even *I* don't know what can be done about it."

True to form, Socrates was determined to help. He cautiously approached the salmon and asked him whether he was okay.

"What do *you* care?" replied the humiliated salmon. "Do you want me to start all over and provide some extended entertainment?"

Socrates knew that the salmon was just venting his frustration and did not take the response personally.

"So your name is Spinner?" Socrates continued.

"No, it's not!" the salmon replied in an angry tone. "My name is Slick! I used to control the entire goings-on of the salmon schools around here, but I guess I ticked a few of them off, because when this lure snagged my tail, no one came to help me. Now they think I'm some nutcase, because of my attempts to remove it. And it's only *just* out of the reach of my jaws. I've become an outcast. Not even those I used to consider good friends come around anymore."

Socrates very kindly let Slick get all of his feelings out before saying anything. When Slick finally slumped in silence, Socrates said, "You know, Slick, two things can come out of a situation like this: you can continue to chase your tail and add to your frustration and humiliation, or you can accept help from someone who wants to help and learn from the experience. I have personally learned over the years that pride and arrogance is what can bring one to the lowest depths of a broken spirit. If that lure was removed from your tail, what would you do?"

Slick pondered the question for some time, and then he looked Socrates in the eye and said, "I think I get your drift."

"Oh, good one!" laughed Socrates. "You get my 'drift.' That's good."

Slick also started chuckling, and it felt good. He had not even so much as smiled in a long time, and now he actually had something to make him laugh.

"Poker!" shouted Socrates. "Let's get to work!"

Slick, in a stunned and sharp response to the name 'Poker,' looked at Socrates and, in a trembling tone, asked, "*You* are Socrates? *The* Socrates? The DK cod?"

Socrates smiled and nodded. "And this guy is my sidekick, Poker. He's known to take on some pretty difficult challenges."

"Yeah, I've heard a few stories," replied Slick.

"Did you hear the one about the whale?" asked Poker.

"No," Slick answered.

"That's because we haven't taken one on yet. But when we *do*, you had better look out!"

Slick looked at Socrates with a smile and said, "He, uh, took on a boat, huh?"

Socrates, detecting Slick's inference, gave him a raised eyebrow, a smile back, and a nod.

"So, let's get to work," blurted out Poker. "By the way, buddy, what exactly are we doing?" Poker had that nearly brain-dead grin on his face as he once more demonstrated his impetuous nature. Slick and Socrates again rolled their eyes in unison and broke out in a light chuckle.

"Okay, now," Socrates started. "Let's see how bad that lure is embedded in Slick's tail."

For a couple of minutes, they examined the lure, and Socrates could see that it had a barb on the hook that kept it from sliding out. They needed to figure out how to remove it. Poker began picking up the vibrations from the engine of a boat. They followed the sound until they could see the boat passing by with a lure following through the water behind it. This was exactly the same situation that had injured Slick before. In a flash of rare brilliance, Poker came up with an idea. He immediately ordered Slick to swim parallel to the lure following the boat. Poker sped alongside Slick and used his bill to hook the shank of the new lure over the shank of the one in Slick's tail. Poker then told Slick to stop abruptly. When Slick suddenly stopped, the line connected to the angler's lure tightened. The angler, detecting a strike, yanked hard, and the lure popped out of Slick's tail.

However, Poker was not through. One of the anglers had his backside hanging over the front of the boat while facing backward and watching the line. Poker grabbed the angler's line just above the lure and swam straight for the boat. The person in the back of the boat detected he had a huge fish hooked, but he could not reel fast enough to tighten the line. Poker swam under the boat and, raising his bill out of the water behind the angler with his backside still hanging over the front of the boat, dropped the lure. It stuck in the angler's pants. When the angler in the back finally tightened his line and went to set the hook, a horrible scream came from the front of the boat; the lure had obviously pierced some flesh. Then, in all the havoc, the angler with the lure in his backside fell off the boat and into the water. Poker was there to greet him with a silent, cold stare. He looked into the angler's eyes with a hard glare, as if to say, *your turn!* In a panic, the angler scrambled back onboard, and the boat bolted out of sight.

Socrates and Slick stared at Poker in disbelief. Poker looked at the two, shrugged, and said, "Hey, what are friends *for?*"

Slick, being the tough fish he had grown up to be, was amazed at the risk Poker had taken on his behalf. Things could have gone wrong. He realized that Poker, without hesitation, was willing to put friendship ahead of possible personal injury. Slick had always taken the easy way out, letting the other fish deal with their own problems, even when it was in his power to help. He felt it toughened them up, which it probably did; however, it had never resulted in any real friendship. The only time anyone responded to him in a positive way was when there was personal advantage in it. Slick felt a total sense of disgust for what he had become, and he openly shared those feelings with Socrates and Poker. After Slick had poured out his heart and profusely thanked Poker for what he had done, Socrates chimed in and stated, "There are such things as new beginnings."

With a curious look, Slick asked, "What are you saying?"

"Well," continued Socrates, "I once heard of a saying that applies to a situation like yours. It goes like this: 'Don't start over again. Start from where you're at.' You obviously have a lot of knowledge and experience from living in this place. Now use it in a positive way. You will benefit not only yourself, but most likely everyone here."

Aunt Dorothy, who by now had caught up to the trio, was discreetly listening in. She was so proud of Socrates and could see why his life was turning into legend. She could not help but enter the conversation and add, "No truer words were ever spoken. I would be honored, Slick, if you would accompany me to our freshwater inlet until you recover. It will also give you a chance to think things through."

Slick was experiencing an extreme surge of humility. He had never known friendship and caring like this before.

He graciously accepted the invitation. Slick then turned to Socrates and Poker.

"When our bay first heard the stories of you two, there was no way I would believe them. Two mavericks, a cod and a swordfish, taking on impossible odds was just too ridiculous to take seriously. Now, I'm beginning to understand. Real friendship can exist when one can see beyond pride and differences."

Socrates and Poker smiled. Socrates then replied to Slick, "However, there is one proper form of pride." Slick looked at him curiously.

Socrates continued. "The form of pride one feels when he is proud to have someone like you in his circle of friends. Take good care of Aunt Dorothy, *friend*."

Slick's whole demeanor suddenly changed, and he started looking like the stately fish he really was. He lifted his head and felt his confidence returning. Now, he decided, his focus would be on helping others.

Chapter Ten

Socrates once more approached Aunt Dorothy. She rubbed her cheek against his and said, "I'm so proud of you. You have done more for this bay in a few weeks than anyone else *ever* has. I really think we will be okay now. I just hope that all of our efforts pay off and that the water in our bay continues to improve."

"It will take a while, Auntie. However, change will happen; there will be a difference, now that everyone in the bay is involved in helping with the problems. It is obvious that the skipper of that boat with the flashing lights is not pleased either. Things will get better. For now, just keep doing what you are doing. Your guidance and love is what will keep this all together." Then, with one last rub of his face against her cheek, he turned and swam away. Of course, he did have one more idea. He just did not want Aunt Dorothy to see his renowned mischievous side. When out of her earshot, he called out to Poker.

"Poker! Go get Billy and the boys! I've got one more idea."

The request did not take long. The blues had been struggling with how to say good-bye to Socrates and Poker, so they were waiting only a short distance away.

"Hey! C'mon, you guys, we need your help!" shouted Poker.

The blues were so excited that they were there in lightning speed.

"Are you ready, boys?" Poker asked excitedly.

"Let's do this thing!" replied Billy. "By the way, what is it we're doing?"

Poker looked at Socrates with that same dumb smile as before. Socrates rolled his eyes, hung his head, and thought, *Great—now Poker has* them *saying it.*

Socrates explained his plan, and immediately the blues raced away. As it turned out, not all of the stinky eels had abandoned the pipes; one of the pipes still had sewage oozing from it. The blues gently rounded up some of the feeding eels in their mouths, being careful not to bite them in half. Then, with Poker and Socrates swimming with them, they located fishing boats from one end of the bay to the other and started attaching the "slithering little stinkys," as they called them, to the anglers' lures. When their task was complete,

Socrates snickered and quipped, "Maybe *now* the fishermen themselves will get a clue."

It did not take long before the anglers were throwing the stinky little critters back into the water, obviously disgusted by the only thing they were catching. All the boats left the bay in a very short time. Poker then looked at Vinny and finally said, "Good job, buddy; you've redeemed yourself."

All of the blues were excited that they had had a chance to share in a little well-intentioned mischief with Socrates and Poker. Poker addressed them.

"I'll miss you guys. But I'll tell you right now"—he hesitated, and they were aching in anticipation of what he was going to say—"you need to eat some lobsters, because your breath really stinks!" The blues busted out laughing, and they swam in circles, holding their sides. Socrates, too, could not help but laugh. This was one of life's savored moments.

As Socrates and Poker said their final good-byes and started cruising out of the bay, Vinny yelled to Poker, "Will we ever see you again?"

"I tell ya what," replied Poker, mimicking the blues' Jersey accent. "How 'bout I drop yous a line?"

Again, laughter exploded through the water as the blues just could not contain their amusement.

Poker looked at Socrates and asked, "Where to now, my friend?"

"South," said Socrates. "Let's head south. I've got a good feeling about this."

AMAYA

Chapter Eleven

For the next few weeks, Socrates and Poker continued lazily south, staying some distance from the shoreline. They were pleasantly surprised by the occasional schools of baitfish, including mackerel that were showing up in this area of the western Atlantic. The mackerel were delicious; however, *catching them* was difficult. This baitfish was incredibly fast, and entire schools could disappear in a heartbeat.

One day, they noticed something that signaled to them to stay away from the largest school of baitfish they had ever seen. Giant tuna were blasting through a huge concentration of mackerel, and large boats were appearing in numbers that neither of them had ever seen at one time. The tuna were the target. One after another, the tuna were fighting the powerful lines baited with mackerel. Unwarily, the tuna would gulp them down in the wild excitement. As the big fish were reeled in ever closer to the boats, huge hooks would pierce their bodies and hoist them over the side. Blood filled the water as the boats took more and more of the powerful fish.

Then, in an instant, everything went calm. The baitfish and the tuna disappeared into the deep.

Socrates and Poker watched all this while staying a safe distance from the boats. The danger from the sheer quantity of boats was intense. Lines and hooks were everywhere. However, about an hour after the fish disappeared, so did the boats.

Wow, thought Socrates. *That was pure insanity*. He could never understand, and he had no way of knowing, why the boats seemed to have such an insatiable need for large fish. Poker then broke the silence.

"Ewww, what *is* that? And it stinks!"

What appeared to be a large, murky slick was floating on the top of the water. It was definitely the source of the horrible smell.

"Where did that come from?" asked Poker.

Socrates surmised that it had to have come from one of the boats; it had emptied its sewage directly into the sea. He was beginning to hate the boats. They contributed nothing to his ocean home—they just took from it and polluted it. The activity of the boats was depressing. However, for now, the two were safe. They had learned valuable lessons over the past several months, which had helped them to survive the perils of this dangerous world.

The following morning, as Socrates and Poker moved a little farther offshore, the most amazing underwater structure came into view. Both of them gasped as they examined the gigantic spires of what appeared to be an underwater palace that continued for miles. Great monoliths jutted up from the seabed to just a little shy of the surface of the water.

"Look at this place!" marveled Socrates. "It's like an underwater kingdom! Where I'm from, there are stories of places like this, but I never dreamed that they actually existed."

The fish in this watery domain were the most diverse and colorful he had ever seen. There were baitfish, rockfish, billfish, and sharks; you name it. The variety of fish was amazing.

"This is beautiful," stated Poker. "What do you say we stay here and rest up a bit?"

"It's okay with me," mumbled Socrates in a dazed tone. "Some exploration of this place could be fun." For days, they examined this surreal world. At every turn, beautiful vistas of rocky formations appeared to be swaying as the ocean plants danced in the gentle currents. The huge variety of fish moved as if directed by the mystic rhythm of an invisible conductor. Socrates then realized, for the first time in his life, that the ocean itself is the conductor; it produces a harmony that causes beauty and peace to exist. Never had he felt so impressed by such intricate balance.

Suddenly, he stammered, "What is that? Who is that?"

Moving through the huge rocky spires was the most beautiful fish he had ever seen. She was gracefully traversing through the spires as though overtaken by the pure ecstasy of living there. Her beauty intrigued Poker, too. She was a tarpon. Her body was silvery and sleek. Her eyes resembled glistening emeralds. Socrates was so enthralled that he blinked his eyes hard, shook his head back and forth, and then refocused on her just to make sure that what he was seeing was real.

"Oh, buddy," blurted out Poker. "You've got it bad!"

"Got *what* bad?" asked Socrates hazily.

"Buddy, I recognize the symptoms. You're lovestruck."

Socrates did not even answer because he could not take his eyes off this enchanting maiden of the sea. She had also noticed Socrates. He was the sheer image of raw power, yet he moved with such dignified confidence. She could not help but be interested in a casual greeting. She smiled and said, "You're new here."

Even her *voice* was beautiful!

"Yes, we are," replied Socrates. "Actually, my friend and I were making our way south when we happened upon this beautiful place."

"It is beautiful, isn't it? I could show you around if you would like a tour."

Socrates did not hesitate to accept the invitation. He was trying hard not to appear too overwhelmed with her beauty.

"A tour would be nice. We have never seen a place quite like this one. By the way, maybe an introduction would be in order?"

She smiled. "Why, of course. My name is Amaya."

Wow, thought Socrates. *A name somehow as beautiful as the girl.*

"That's a very pretty name," he replied.

This time, her smile reflected a graceful acceptance of the compliment.

"My name is Socrates, and this is my friend Poker."

Her eyes suddenly opened wide, and she swam back a few feet. She looked at the two of them and excitedly responded, "You're them! The ones we have been hearing about! You're the DK cod and the swordfish! Everyone has been telling stories of you two for months. I've personally thought it was a little of a stretch to believe the account of the attack on the boat and the shark, though."

Socrates and Poker said nothing. They simply glanced at each other with smiles that cloaked their experiences of mutual encounters with danger.

"Well, you know what they say," replied Socrates coyly. "You can't believe everything you hear."

For hours, Amaya showed Socrates and Poker areas of this underwater realm that were so intriguing that words couldn't come close to describing them. Some of the most fascinating sights were the coral reefs, which sparkled with dazzling beauty when the sun was high in the sky. However, when night fell, a quivering fear of danger from the unknown gripped one with suspense. The cliff walls and monoliths contained plants and shellfish of every color and variety. Everything enchantingly danced back and forth with the gentle currents. Then, in the morning, as the sun shone and the wind kicked up ripples on the surface of the water, millions of tiny sunrays joined in the dance as they flickered off the underwater life. All of this left Socrates and Poker speechless for a long time. They continued their tour in a prolonged trance.

"And it's different every day," Amaya said, as she purposely broke the silence. *After all*, she thought, *how do you get to know someone if there is no conversation?*

A loud voice interrupted Amaya's attempt to speak to Socrates. "Poker!

Out of nowhere appeared a school of swordfish. Their leader blurted out, "Wow, buddy, you have been leaving an interesting trail!" It was Jacko, and he was overly excited. "We saw and talked to Aunt Dorothy and Slick a few weeks ago, and they mentioned you were heading south. We decided to try to catch up to see what you two are up to now. You and Socrates really helped things in the bay up north. The fishing boats have not been around for at least a couple of weeks. The people on the boats with the flashing lights have been lowering some weird-looking devices into the water. Maybe they got your clue, if you know what I mean. The stinky pipes where the eels hung out are now gone. Maybe your little episode of attaching the eels to the fishing lines left a bad taste in someone's mouth. Everyone is telling the story about you dropping the lure in the angler's pants. The story is getting a little wilder every time, but it sure has stirred everyone's imaginations about what to do to help the bay's situation. Aunt Dorothy now has Slick taking the lead in coordinating the schools of fish through her freshwater inlet. Everyone looks and feels so much better."

"Hey, Jacko?" replied Poker. "*Breathe*, buddy! You're going too fast!"

Jacko, with an embarrassed smile on his face, said, "We just miss you, pal!"

"We miss you guys, too," laughed Poker. "How would you like to hang around with us for a little while? This is Amaya. She has been helping us explore this beautiful place. She lives here."

Amaya had taken an awkward position of almost hiding behind Socrates. She now perceived that all the stories about Socrates and Poker were actually true. Socrates turned around, raised his eyes, and, looking directly at Amaya, started the introductions. The swordfish were mesmerized at Amaya's beauty; never had they seen such a fish. Amaya was pure elegance, grace, and beauty.

Their trancelike staring at Amaya embarrassed Poker, who waved his fin in front of Jacko's face.

"Ocean to Jacko! Ocean to Jacko! Come *in*, Jacko!"

Jacko blinked and snapped out of his daze. "Amaya, it is a pleasure to meet you. Are you sure there's no problem with us staying a little while?"

The rest of the swordfish looked as if they were ready to *beg* for the opportunity to stay, when Amaya answered that it would be a privilege to have them.

Jacko approached Poker and asked, "Does she have a sister?"

Poker laughed and assured his friend that with so many fish in the area, finding someone to hang out with should not be too difficult. However, even Poker doubted there would be anyone else found with Amaya's beauty and grace.

BONDAR   UNCLE GNARLS

Chapter Twelve

The next few days were fun. Socrates, Poker, Amaya, and the swordfish raced through Amaya's domain with wild abandon. They were darting in and out of the reefs, the monoliths, the rock piles, and everywhere else one could explore. They were also playing all sorts of games that were a wonderful break from the monotony of constantly looking for baitfish. However, baitfish was always plentiful and close by when they *did* get hungry.

On the fourth day, an ominous creature started silently scouring the area. It caught the immediate attention of

Socrates. He, Poker, and Amaya were resting near a deep rock pile. The huge, strange-looking shark seemed motionless between the sea and the sun.

"What is that?" asked Socrates.

"It's a hammerhead," responded Amaya. "It's roundup time."

Her voice was quivering, and rightly so. She explained what a roundup was: For the next hour, hundreds of hammerhead sharks would start out in a very wide area. Each shark would menacingly scare tarpon into a smaller and smaller space. Through sheer panic, the tarpon would school together by the thousands into what appeared to be a giant swirling vortex. Then the hammerheads, when it was apparent there was no escape for the tarpon, would attack and gorge themselves. Now Amaya was sobbing as she completed her explanation of the horror of the event.

"They're going to decimate us again!" she cried.

Socrates nestled his face next to hers and, with a defiant look, said, "Not this time!"

Socrates was angry, yet, he was wise enough to know that anger was an emotion that clouded common sense. He had to keep cool and try to figure out a way to stop the carnage and make sure that this sort of thing did not happen again. There seemed only one way, and it was going to require self-sacrificing courage—on the parts of *everyone* involved. He knew the plan would invoke a level of fear in all the participants, but he also knew that fear itself could be an asset, as it could help keep expectation in check. This was about helping others; by keeping that goal in mind, self-preservation would not be an issue distracting the players.

Socrates started by discussing his plan with Poker, Amaya, and Jacko. As dangerous as it sounded, they responded without reservation. Socrates ordered Jacko to gather every swordfish within at least a hundred miles. Jacko and his group scattered in every direction in immediate reaction to the orders. Amaya chimed in with a way to round up thousands of barracuda. Their strong jaws and teeth were going to be strategic to the plan. Poker was going to coordinate the activity of the tarpon, which were going to be the bait to spring the trap.

It was already late in the afternoon, but no one wasted any time gathering the forces necessary for what was shaping up to be the largest battle of its kind anyone had ever heard of. Excitement gripped Poker, Amaya, and Jacko; however, Socrates told the three of them to just gather everyone necessary and not breathe a word of the plan. He would give everyone instructions when the time was right. He did not want details of the plan to come to the attention of the hammerheads.

Finally, Socrates, thinking back fondly to his need for Leo the dogfish, asked Amaya: "Who is the most ominous and fearsome creature in this entire area?"

She looked at Socrates with her own hint of mischief in her smile. She had no idea what Socrates was thinking, but she knew that, whatever it was, the hammerheads were in for the scare of their lives. She said nothing but quickly swam away toward a deep cavern that was off limits to all fish. She returned, later that day, with her tutor. He was the one who had taught her what she had needed to know about the wonderful balance of this underwater utopia. Amaya approached Socrates and introduced her wise teacher.

"Socrates," grinned Amaya, "I would like to introduce you to Uncle Gnarls."

Amaya moved out of the way, and the biggest moray eel Socrates had ever seen slithered into view. As he moved toward Socrates, Uncle Gnarls yawned and asked why he had been disturbed from his nap. His mouth opened wide, and the huge, jagged teeth and powerful jaws that made up the bulk of his giant head came into clear view. Socrates shuddered, but he knew he could not appear scared. He approached Uncle Gnarls and introduced himself. His voice was wavering a little; Uncle Gnarls was absolutely the scariest creature he had ever seen in his life. He felt relieved to know that Uncle Gnarls was a close friend of Amaya.

"Uncle, I need to discuss with you the problem of the hammerheads and this so-called roundup. Would you mind if I took a little of your time to discuss a plan that I've come up with?"

Uncle Gnarls agreed to listen, provided his student, Amaya, could join in. Socrates certainly had no problem with that.

The three discussed the details of the operation against the hammerheads, and Uncle Gnarls had some important insight to offer. "For one thing," he said, "this mission cannot result in the destruction of the hammerheads. Their presence is necessary in order to keep the ocean clean. Sharks clean up carcasses of dead creatures, including even those of whales. Without the presence of the hammerheads and other sharks like them, the entire balance of the ocean would be upset. The effects of their absence would be worse than what is happening with the pollution coming from the boats and the dumping. In addition, if this plan is successful, maybe an important message can be sent to the polluters as well."

Uncle Gnarls, with his seriously toothy overbite, got a look on his face reminiscent of Amaya's mischievous grin.

Uh-oh, thought Socrates. *I can hardly wait to hear what he's got in mind.*

However, Uncle Gnarls kept whatever he was thinking to himself for the time being and began reviewing the details of the matter at hand. He appreciated Socrates' strong constitution and his willingness to help. Uncle Gnarls had also heard the stories about Socrates and Poker, and from his conversation with Socrates, he had no problem believing what he had heard. Uncle Gnarls looked at Amaya and, noticing her obvious interest in Socrates, gave her a wink of approval. She blushed, and her eyes twinkled. Uncle Gnarls also noticed a small ripple in the water; her heart had fluttered. In his wisdom, he did not say a thing.

After they finalized the plan, Poker rounded up all the participants. Socrates then laid out their instructions. The immediate need was to make sure that everyone agreed to his or her personal assignment; they had to be determined to make this work. All of them, of course, were excited to join in; this plan was necessary in order to restore balance to their world.

Chapter Thirteen

The following morning as dawn approached, the tarpon started on their scamper to capture the notice of the hammerheads. The directive was to keep the sharks as close to the monoliths, which would provide a natural cover for the swordfish and the barracuda, as possible. The tarpon worked it well, darting back and forth to give the illusion of panic and confusion. For hours, they worked from a large circumference, continually tightening their ranks. The hammerheads must have thought that they had become masters of the roundup because it was going so smoothly, and they grinned with evil pleasure. They saw the tarpon grouping closer and closer together. The trap was now set.

Tarpon by the thousands had formed an extremely tight, spinning vortex that made escape seem impossible; their vulnerability was now at its peak. Then, suddenly, it happened: The hammerheads, following the signal from their leader, lunged into the middle of the vortex. However, they focused only on the tarpon—they did not even notice the swordfish and barracuda that had encircled them. As the hammerheads lunged into the middle of the tarpon vortex, the tarpon, on queue and with perfect timing, scattered. That is when the swordfish, led by Poker, slammed into the sides of each hammerhead. Two swordfish, one on either side, in perfect unison hit each hammerhead hard. One thing about hammerheads is that their brains short-circuit if grabbed simultaneously by both sides of their hammer; it is almost as if they lose their thought function. The barracuda, working in pairs, moved in. In unison, they bit down on each side of the sharks' hammers and hung on. The battle to subdue all of the hammerheads, which were greatly outnumbered, went on for hours. The hammerheads were hurting badly and in a state of panic. The swordfish and barracuda started escorting them to a common area. However, their leader, Bondar, was being stubbornly defiant. Socrates had pinpointed him from the beginning as the one orchestrating the attack on the tarpon. Socrates motioned to Poker and the barracuda whom he had assigned to capture the leader of the hammerheads to escort Bondar to a special area isolated from the other sharks. Socrates then approached the giant shark and sharply stated: "It's over, pal!"

"Don't bet on it!" Bondar replied. "We'll regroup, and then you'll see who the masters of this ocean are!"

Bondar did not see Uncle Gnarls silently approaching from behind. However, as the giant eel, who was easily as long as Bondar and almost as thick around, came into view, Bondar's eyes almost popped out of his hammers.

"Uncle Gnarls," said Socrates, "have you ever wondered what one of those eyes on the end of the hammer tastes like?"

"It's one thing I haven't *yet* had the pleasure of eating—but it looks pretty tasty." Uncle Gnarls's eyes narrowed to slits.

"Why don't you try one now? I'm curious about the flavor."

Uncle Gnarls circled the shark with a menacing grin on his face. He approached Bondar from the front to give him the complete scope of what was about to happen. Bondar tried to squirm away, but the barracuda just bit down harder, which kept him paralyzed. When Uncle Gnarls opened his mouth and the full effect of his teeth and jaws were impressed upon the shark, Bondar shrieked, "No! Please! Noooo!"

"So," exclaimed Socrates, "are you interested in an agreement, or are we going to be entertained by what sharks will do, even to one of their own who's swimming around blind and wounded?" Socrates voice was bold and angry; after all, Amaya's family and friends were the ones the sharks had threatened. Bondar reluctantly complied. He had hoped, however, in his stubborn pride and in order to save face, that none of the other hammerheads had heard him scream. This was the moment of his greatest humiliation: inferior creatures had defeated him. Socrates motioned to the barracuda to release their grip. If they had bitten down any harder, they would have pierced Bondar's optic nerves, which would have blinded him instantly. He was bleeding from the puncture wounds and visibly shaken and embarrassed.

"Now are you ready to discuss with us what your problem is?" Socrates questioned in a sharp tone. Bondar nodded. Socrates then dismissed everyone except Poker, Amaya, and Uncle Gnarls.

"So," continued Socrates, "explain what this is all about!"

"It wasn't always like this," began Bondar. "There used to be so many baitfish schools that we had no problem finding plenty of food when we weren't feeding on the carcass of a dead whale or some large fish. The big fish used to be so plentiful that there were plenty of dead fish remains for us to eat without ever touching the baitfish schools. However, as the large-carcass numbers declined, we had to target the baitfish. The boats have been taking more and more big fish with their nets, and we are simply not fast enough to chase the little fish individually. Therefore, we started targeting the tarpon in a roundup out of sheer survival necessity. The tarpon are fast, but they are large, and our chances at a meal increase when they are crowded together. That's it." Bondar, who had been face-to-face with Socrates and Amaya, shamefully turned away.

This explanation however, had helped all of them to see things from the sharks' perspective. No one spoke for a while. They were pondering Bondar's candid justification for the hammerheads' actions.

Uncle Gnarls finally broke the silence. He looked Bondar in the eyes and, in a firm voice, said, "It stops here and now!"

Bondar's countenance was softening as he considered, for the first time, Amaya's perception. She had not even said anything, but he had been able to read her expressions and body language during his explanation. She was now shuddering while thinking about everyone she knew who had fallen victim to Bondar and the hammerheads during the last roundup.

"I'm sorry," Bondar finally said to Amaya, with his head hung in disgrace. "I'm really sorry." Then he turned to Uncle Gnarls and Socrates and asked, "What, then, do we do? We need food!"

"I think we now understand your dilemma," replied Socrates. "And for some reason, I'm guessing that Uncle Gnarls has an idea." Socrates had been watching Uncle

Gnarls's reaction to Bondar's response and detected that he had something in mind. Uncle Gnarls smiled and then looked at Bondar.

"You, my friend," said Uncle Gnarls, "are going to get a chance to restore your dignity and redeem yourself. Once this little episode is over, we will make sure you have plenty to eat. In fact, what we are going to do is bound to get some serious attention by those responsible for polluting our watery home and causing these problems, so perhaps things will start improving. Are you up for this, Bondar? Things are going to get a bit stinky."

Bondar was feeling an unexpected reversal of his nasty disposition. For the first time in years, his ever-present scowl turned into a favorable smile.

Poker then blurted out, "And when this is over, I'll probably need to find you some lobsters—it sounds like you're going to need some! By the way, Uncle Gnarls, what is it we're doing?"

Socrates could not help laughing. "You're an idiot," he said.

As usual, Poker just hovered there with that big brain-dead smile on his face.

Chapter Fourteen

Uncle Gnarls wasted no time. The sooner this escapade was over the sooner the hammerheads would get to eat. Some of the swordfish took off to find one of the big, foul-smelling, oily sewage slicks that were being noticed lately. Others went to find one of the boats that were using mile-long drift nets, which had become more common recently. The nets were cruel; they would trap and kill every fish and ocean mammal in their path. Large rockfish were to collect as much seaweed as possible. Small rockfish were going to be the weavers.

Socrates was finally getting the picture; it was pure genius. Poker did not even really think about it; he just darted off for a little while, making arrangements of his own. In addition, Amaya was organizing the barracuda for something special to take place when the event was over.

It took only about an hour for a smelly sewage slick to be located. Not much later, a boat that had just let out its mile-long net was sighted. Uncle Gnarls then called the hammerheads together and explained the plan. Quickly, the sharks sprang into action. In groups, they grabbed the net on either end. The hammerheads were stacked, one on top of the other; this allowed them to control the extreme weight. With the net firmly grasped in their teeth, they followed the swordfish's directions and slowly encircled the horrible sludge. As they were moving, the ends of the net grew ever closer, forming a complete circle around the mass of filth. The rockfish then started spreading out evenly with the seaweed in their mouths. The little ones, the weavers, would then grab the ends of pieces of the plants and weave them in and out, from top to bottom, to close the openings in the net. The activity went on for hours. The hammerheads finally finished encircling the horrible mass, and the rockfish completed closing and securing the ends of the net. Then Uncle Gnarls gave the order for another group of hammerheads to draw the bottom of the net together for the weavers to tie off. When the work was finished, everyone regrouped and anxiously awaited the reeling-in of the net by those on the boat.

All of the fish were very proud of what they had accomplished together and were laughing as they imagined what the fishermen's response would be. Hours went by with anxiety building; finally, they saw the boat returning, approaching the net. A huge cable was lowering into the water. It attached to a large device on the boat that started the process of reeling in the "catch." As the landed part of the net swayed overhead, the net started spilling all the horrible sewage onto the deck of the boat! Deckhands were hanging their heads off the side, heaving and coughing. They were so sick that they could not even manage to stop the automated equipment that just kept reeling the putrid filth onto the boat. Within a few hours, the awful mass in the net was completely out of the water. The deckhands could do nothing about it; all of their equipment was jammed and broken, because no one had been able to control it. The boat took off at full speed with all of the horrible mass of filth gracing the deck. The weaving of the seaweed had held, and the plan had worked flawlessly.

All of the fish were ecstatic. They were laughing and congratulating each other for their individual efforts. The hammerheads were even spending time acknowledging the rockfish, including the little guys who had done the weaving of the seaweed. Bondar simply looked around in wonder as the celebration went on; never had he experienced this unity among such a diverse group. One little rockfish, one of the weavers, swam up to Bondar and introduced himself.

"Hi, I'm Peetie. What you did was amazing. You are so strong. Can you tell me what it was like hauling that net in your jaws?" Peetie was excited to have the opportunity to talk to someone like Bondar, who was seemingly larger than life. Bondar smiled at Peetie.

"Why not? Let's talk some story."

Just then, though, Poker busted into the scene and commanded, in a loud voice, "All of you hammers, front, and center!"

The hammerheads, in immediate response, grouped together. Bondar swam to the front and asked Poker, "What's this about?" Poker and Bondar were only a few feet apart, and as soon as Bondar opened his mouth, Poker's eyes went dramatically crossed, and he rolled over backward, pretending to pass out. He then refocused on Bondar and said, "Ewww, your breath *stinks*!" Then he signaled with a nod, and hundreds of rockfish raced up to the hammerheads with at least two huge lobsters for each of them to feast on.

"Chew it up well, now! It will help with that bad taste in your mouth!" shouted Poker.

Socrates smiled big as he remembered Poker's problem with the eels served up to him by Vinny Blue. The hammerheads seemed to be enjoying the lobsters as much as Poker had. They were slowly chewing and savoring the sweetness, and the shell helped scrape the inside of their mouths clean of the oily muck that had penetrated through their teeth while maneuvering the net. The impact of all that was happening was obviously having a positive effect on the sharks; they were now feeling that they were not just a lone species, doomed to roam in lonesome packs terrorizing everyone, and they now felt a sense of purpose and freedom. Socrates watched Bondar as the hammerhead leader sat in silent reflection. Socrates swam up to him.

"Feels good, doesn't it?" he asked.

Bondar answered, with a sigh of relief, "It feels *real* good."

Uncle Gnarls then broke in and announced, "Everyone, let's head home." It was an amazing sight to see: Thousands of fish had gathered to celebrate the occasion. The swordfish were talking and laughing with the hammerheads, the rockfish with the swordfish, and every combination of fish were making friends. It was the most satisfying result Socrates could have ever imagined. However, the day was not over. They all arrived back at Amaya's beautiful domain, where thousands of barracuda, who had prepared a massive meal of mackerel and herring for the hammerheads, greeted them. Uncle Gnarls looked at Amaya with pride and said, "I was wondering what you were doing."

Amaya smiled and invited the hammerheads to eat. The sharks paused in stunned silence, glancing back and forth at each other and wondering if this was for real.

"C'mon," urged Amaya. "Eat up."

The hammerheads then did start eating, but they were being careful, for once, to control themselves and their ravenous hunger. This time, they had an air of dignity about them; after all, their host was Amaya, "the princess of the sea."

Chapter Fifteen

The huge gathering lasted well into the night, and only the barracuda, after saying their good-byes, actually left; everyone else drifted off to rest until the next morning. At dawn, Uncle Gnarls sought out Socrates, Amaya, and Poker for a private meeting. They discussed everything from the problems with the boats and nets to the dwindling stocks of baitfish and the quality of the water in certain regions. Some of it, nothing could be done about, but they did come to an accord on the things they could control. Uncle Gnarls then asked Poker to call Bondar to join in the meeting. Bondar was pleased that his input could be of value. Finally, they all made a decision after some discussion and everyone's insights.

Bondar, as leader of the hammerheads, would patrol what everyone was now calling "Amaya's Kingdom." With dignity and grace, Amaya accepted the official appointment as princess of the domain. The hammerheads also accepted the opportunity to accompany teams of barracuda when they located schools of baitfish. The hammerheads would then be getting enough to eat. In addition, the barracuda would report any large fish or whale carcass found so that the hammerheads could also take advantage of that food source (after all, barracuda move much faster than hammerheads and can cover great distances in only a short time). Additionally, all issues regarding problems were hereafter going to Uncle Gnarls for his consideration and decision. As for Socrates and Poker, they both felt a deep sense of satisfaction at having seen so much accomplishment in a few short days. At the urging of Amaya and Uncle Gnarls, they decided to extend their visit, awaiting the warmer currents before continuing their trek south. At least that appeared to Socrates to be a perfect justification for staying. His real motivation was to spend more time with Amaya; no one else had ever enlivened his spirit as she had.

Amaya had a surprise for Poker. That same afternoon, after excusing herself for a little while, she returned with a friend. Poker was busy chatting with Bondar when Amaya approached him and said, "Poker, I want to introduce you to someone."

From behind Amaya emerged the most gorgeous young swordfish Poker had ever seen. He gulped, feeling a bit awkward; after all, this was a total surprise. He glanced at Bondar with a half smile and then reengaged his eyes on the swordfish.

"Poker," Amaya continued, "this is Serine. Serine, this is Poker."

Poker was at a loss. Never before that day, had he experienced an introduction to a female fish who was interested in him.

"H-H-Hello," stammered Poker. "My name's—well, uh—*Poker.*" He felt so stupid. After all, she already knew his name.

Socrates was snickering in the background. *Nothing changes with this guy*, he thought.

Serine, graciously, replied, "It's nice to meet you, Poker. I have been hearing a lot about you. Would you mind sharing some stories with me?"

Poker smiled coyly and answered, "Well, why don't you tell me what you've heard, and I'll make some other stuff up. How's that?" They both laughed and started swimming away together. Bondar then called out to Poker, "Ooh, you've got it bad!"

"Watch it, buddy," retorted Poker. "My *orders* were to ram you, not pierce you through—if you get my drift."

Bondar suddenly realized how fortunate he was. He had not given much thought to the restraint exercised by the swordfish at the roundup; they could have easily finished off the hammerheads. However, that had not been the operation's intent; it had been to gain control of a bad situation. The wisdom in the plan, as constructed by Uncle Gnarls, had been to use this event to achieve a mutual commitment to balance their world—*not* to destroy any more of it. Bondar was feeling good about his own contribution that had made all of this work. He no longer felt like an aimless wanderer; he now belonged somewhere and could use his past to help others with the same feelings, to help them realize their natural place in this watery world of never-ending wonder. Bondar silently approached Uncle Gnarls and started sharing his thoughts. Uncle Gnarls was pleased with Bondar's comprehension; he was going to be a welcome addition to Amaya's Kingdom.

A tiny voice piped in.

"Well, how about *me*? Can I help?" It was little Peetie. He had been following Bondar since the previous day. "I never did get to hear your story about the net. Can we talk about it now?"

Bondar smiled. This little fish was as small as a herring, but his spirit had no limits.

Uncle Gnarls raised an eyebrow, gave Bondar a look, and said, "Here's your first opportunity to make a difference, tutor."

Bondar understood Uncle Gnarls's hint—he now had his first assignment as a teacher. He looked at the little fish with a smile and said, "Sure, Peetie. Why don't we spend the rest of the day together, and we will share some stories, how's that sound?"

Little Peetie was so excited that he did about twenty backflips. He excitedly responded, "This day is going to be *so* awesome! Follow me, and I'll show you a cool place where we can share our stories."

Bondar then humbly set out—a giant shark following his tiny escort to a favorite place.

Chapter Sixteen

Uncle Gnarls, who was seriously in need of some rest, silently departed, disappearing into the depths of his mysterious cavern. Socrates and Amaya reflected on everything that had happened over the past few days. It was hard for either of them to comprehend the wisdom that Uncle Gnarls had displayed in the face of a seemingly impossible situation. They both recognized that the success of the operation was not Uncle Gnarls's reaction to the problem with the hammerheads; success had come from his restraint, not from overreacting to the problem. Socrates looked into Amaya's eyes.

"We still have a lot to learn, don't we?"

Before Amaya could reply, seemingly out of nowhere, a huge storm set in. Rain started pouring hard over the surface of the ocean. Amaya glanced up and then back at Socrates, smiled, and asked, "Do you want to add to the list of how much *everyone* has to learn?"

Socrates gave her a silent, questioning gaze.

"Come with me!" she said, and she turned and quickly raced to the surface. He followed.

"Hurry—stick your head up out of the water, and feel the rain on your face!"

The two, in unison, elevated their heads above the surface and held them there for about two full minutes. The rain felt soft, cleansing, and refreshing. Socrates had never experienced such a restorative feeling of unsoiled purity in his life; it was utter bliss. Then, as their clean, smooth, soft faces slid back below the surface, Socrates found himself again at a loss for words. However, gracious and beautiful Amaya, with her emerald green eyes sparkling like stars, looked at handsome Socrates and added, "Yes, we still *do* have a lot to learn. I think that if our ocean ever gets to feeling as pure as this wonderful rain, our entire world will finally have a chance to achieve its perfect balance."

Socrates could manage only a nod. He had started tearing up at the sudden thought of his precious sister, Mara—how he wished that she could be in this moment with him! He knew that Mara would have loved Amaya as much he did. He gazed overhead at the clearing, blue sky with all its beautiful, billowing clouds. He thought about what he and his new friends had accomplished since Mara's death and how he was honoring her memory by maintaining a firm resolve to find solutions to problems the creatures in their world were facing. He felt strong and even more determined to finish what he had started. Slowly, he swam over to Amaya, gently rubbed his cheek against hers, smiled, and, with a look of adventure in his eyes, said, "Tell me, what's so mysterious about Uncle Gnarls's cavern?"